BANGED

BY THE

BIKERS

LOLITA MINX

eXplicitTales

CONTENTS

BANGED BY THE BIKERS

PART 1

It was a lousy cafe in a sleazy part of town. The good news was that it paid weekly. Right now, new in town, that was important. Later maybe I'd be able to find a better job, one with decent pay, but when you have no job history and no particular skills, you can't be fussy. I'd taken the first thing I was offered—something to pay the bills.

The first day I put on the uniform, a smiley face, and my best attitude. Having a friendly demeanor was supposed to ensure I got decent tips. At least that's what Al, the owner, said. Of course, he had his own reasons for wanting the help to be friendly. The food was shitty and he needed friendly waitresses if he expected customers to come back and spend more money.

I'm not sure what I expected, but it quickly became apparent that most of the customers belonged in this neighborhood. They were as down-market as it was. That made sense, of course. Who crossed town to eat at a shitty diner? That they were locals unfortunately destroyed my dreams of decent tips. Even if they had money, they didn't seem like big tippers, this assortment of street thugs, local store owners, and some bikers who hung out at the motorcycle repair shop right across the street.

Overall, it was a scruffy slice of humanity who wandered in to drink the overheated coffee or a soft drink, and wolf down sandwiches, with coleslaw or fries—a description that fairly comprehensively covered the entire menu.

The gang members seemed to be all from the same gang and behaved fairly well, considering. Actually, I'd known enough guys like them at school not to be impressed by their baggy pants and dislike for wearing a baseball cap as if you knew the bill marked its front.

The bikers were a rough lot, and being around them was a new experience. I found them exciting in a nasty, sexy kind of way. Some of the guys were just greasy dirt bags but some were hot. One guy particular, in his twenties and obviously some kind of leader, caught my eye. He wore jeans and a vest. His muscular shoulders were covered with lurid tattoos of animals, a dancing girl and unfamiliar patterns.

"Hey new girl, my name's Scotty," he said when I came over to the booth to take their order.

"I'm Carla."

He looked up at my name tag. "I can see that."

"He can see you have nice tits, too." This from one of

his buddies, a large black man who wore a handkerchief around his head, pirate style.

"She does have nice tits, Scotty. I'll bet they are tasty." This from a squat white guy, who also sported a variety of tattoos, including a spider on his cheek.

The comments were crude, but the guys were being friendly. "I'll take that as a compliment." Truth is, I was flattered. It's nice when good-looking guys notice.

I took their order, put it in, and then scurried around serving other customers. When I came back to their table carrying their food, I had to reach past Scotty to hand the other guys their orders. I felt his hand gently stroke my bare leg. The blood rushed to my head.

He smiled. "Hey Carla, how about going for a ride with me later? Have you ever been on big bike, roaring down an open road? I swear it can make your blood boil."

All kinds of crazy tingling sensations were running through me. Maybe my blood was already near a boil.

"I have to work."

When he laughed I was taken by the musical quality of his freely flowing laughter. "This dump closes at ten. How about a midnight run?"

It sounded exciting, exhilarating. It sounded too good; he was moving too fast.

"Maybe another time."

I was relieved when he smiled and didn't get upset. I had found the idea more attractive than I'd let on. Once I got my bearings, if he was as nice as he seemed, it would be fun to take him up on it. With the reputations bikers have, it seemed like a good idea to get to know this one better before I let him drag me off somewhere alone. On the other hand, I didn't like missing out entirely. I didn't want him thinking I wouldn't consider it, just that I couldn't now. That left things open ended.

Shortly after that I got caught up in a mini rush hour with new customers, mostly construction workers who were repaving the next street over, came in for the dinner hour.

"Watch them sleazy bikers," a middle-aged man sitting at the counter said as I walked over to refill my coffee pot. The free refill policy kept customers, even with the rotten coffee, but it also made a lot of work for the waitresses. People who are promised something free get pretty insistent about getting it.

I stopped and topped up his cup, figuring he was looking for attention. "What do you mean?"

"That scum will take advantage. A pretty girl like you should be real careful."

"They're okay. They aren't causing me a problem."

"They will, given half a chance. Less than half."

BANGED BY THE BIKERS

Scotty's group called for their check and I took it to them.

"Another night for that ride then?"

"We'll see." I smiled. Maybe I was doing this right. I like that he never asked if I had a boyfriend. I guessed he didn't give a rat's ass if I did or not. That was kind of exciting too.

The three bikers paid their bill and left, heading back across the street. I watched them go, thinking that Scotty was really hot. The others were interesting too, but Scotty was something special. Just looking at him got my heart pounding. Being alone with him might be a whole different thing than scary.

The man frowned. "I guess you must be one of them women that thinks those bad boys are hot. It's all that television shit makes 'em seem glamorous. They're just bums and mean trouble."

He as starting to piss me off. "I can take care of myself."

He scowled fiercely. "You think so?"

I just glared back at him.

Shortly after that he paid his bill and left. I looked at the clock. Two more hours until end of shift, before I could go home.

I sighed, remembering that home meant half a bottle of

a decent wine sitting on the table in my apartment, a package of hot dogs, a bag of chips and television. I was beginning to think that turning down that midnight ride had been a stupid play. But to an extent that asshole at the counter was right—those bikers could be trouble.

When the shift ended, I was tired but reasonably pleased. Only time would tell if this new life was going to be better than my old one.

———◆———

I walked alone out of the diner into a dark street. Al was inside doing some bookkeeping and locking up the booze. The other waitress worked an overlapping shift. She got off right after dinner. In the dark, the distance to the bus stop seemed a much longer walk than it had in the daylight.

I saw a few lights flickered dimly inside the motorcycle repair shop across the street, but the big garage doors were down and shut for the evening. Everything was closed at this time of night. Standing there fretting about shit wasn't doing me any good. I took a deep breath and started walking briskly, realizing that I had no idea when the next bus arrived. I didn't know the schedule yet.

It was too late to do much about that.

BANGED BY THE BIKERS

I walked past cars parked along street, past a bum sleeping in the doorway of a shuttered and abandoned store, and on toward the bus stop.

"You shouldn't walk around her alone at night."

I turned and saw the man from the cafe, the one who had lectured me about the bikers earlier. "What are you doing here?"

"Waiting for you."

"I told you to leave me alone."

"You said you could take care of yourself. It so happens I like feisty women, women who think they can stop me."

He didn't look like much, but that guy moved surprisingly fast. He had me by the arm and jerked me into the alley. I started to scream for help, and he slapped me, cutting it short. Then he pinned me against the wall and was tearing at my clothes and muttering about goddam whores. I fought back, scratching and kicking. I must have hurt him because he suddenly roared, and punched me in the stomach, taking the wind out of me.

I collapsed to the ground.

"Here is fine with me."

I looked up. He was undoing his pants and grinning. Then a scowl replaced the grin, and I saw a swirl of motion, heard a scuffle.

Hands scooped me up. Men's voices asked me questions, but I couldn't make out the words. "You're safe now," someone said.

I passed out.

I woke to find myself in the biker's arms—Scotty's arms. We sat on a couch. The black man sat in a chair drinking a beer. The squat man was coming over to us with a bowl and washcloth. The water was warm and Scotty used his free hand to wash my face with an amazing gentleness.

The squat man sat on the floor, watching. "That guy won't bother you again."

"He won't bother anyone for quite some time," the black man said.

"When you fainted we brought you to our little hiding place."

I felt safe in Scotty's embrace, but his closeness also made me tremble. He was a strong, exciting man and I was alone in his place, my clothes torn. My trembling was arousal—I'd never been in such an odd, yet erotic situation.

Scotty looked into my eyes and I felt something magic pass between us. It held me motionless as he leaned forward to kiss me in a long and tender kiss that quickly grew hot. His hand moved up under my top; his fingers touched my breasts, sending shock waves through me that teased my nipples hard.

When we broke the kiss the other guys were watching Scotty fondling me. His breath grew ragged and I knew he wanted this to go further. I did too. It felt too good to want him to stop, but the watching eyes put a chill on things.

"Scotty," I managed.

He smiled. "Do you want me to take you home?"

I looked in those eyes again and felt a shiver of desire. "No." I nodded toward his friend.

He stood and held out a hand. Numbly, I took it. He pulled me to my feet and led me into another room.

It was insane. After what had happened, I wanted him to fuck me. I want him more than I'd ever wanted anyone.

———◆———

The room held little more than a dresser and a low bed—a mattress on the floor. "Home sweet home," Scotty said, sitting down, pulling me down beside him. I lost my balance and I fell on my back and he moved over me, smothering my reason in hot kisses as his hands pulled my top up over my breasts.

I caught my breath as he brought his hot lips to my

nipples, kissing and sucking them, making them grow erect. The world went into a tumble. I felt his tongue trace hot lines over my stomach, his hands under my skirt, working my panties down my hips. I'd never been with such an aggressive guy, a man who took what he wanted, didn't give me a chance to think.

"Oh so sweet," he said. He had my panties off and spread my legs apart to give my naked pussy a hungry look that made me wet. He thrust his face down to lick my cunt, running the lovely hot creature inside me and up between my nether lips, making my clitoris quiver and I gasped.

He rose up on his knees and fumbled with my skirt, getting it off me. "I want you naked," he said. He sat me upright to jerk my top over my head and pull it off releasing me to flop back on his bed, enjoying the lusty way he drank in my naked body.

His smile showed his hunger as he knelt, undoing his pants and pushing them down. The sight of his hard cock jutting out was beautiful, hot, and it was big enough to be a bit intimidating. Then his arms slipped under my bare legs, lifting them, tipping me back and my cunt up toward that stiff prick. I watched, riveted, unable to take my eye off the sight of that throbbing shaft as he moved forward, pushing the head between the lips of my pussy, spreading it open.

Then he leaned into me, his weight burying that cock in me, making me cry out. My eyes opened wide as he impaled me. When his pelvis pressed against the backs of my legs, he held still, kissing me, forcing his tongue in my mouth. As his tongue explored my mouth, he began fucking me hard, ramming that cock into me.

Finally he broke the kiss allowing me to squeal with pleasure at each thrust, each penetration of my cunt. Delirious with pleasure, I reached my hands out to caress his muscular, tattooed shoulders as he powered into me.

———◆———

Scotty was caught up in fucking me, his attention buried deep inside my pussy with his hard cock. Over his shoulder I saw his buddies standing in the doorway, watching and smiling. And then Scotty came, shooting his cum inside me.

When he sat up it left me completely exposed to their stares. "Your friends…"

Scott nodded and sat up, letting his hands run down my belly. I lay still as he stroked my pussy. I felt his cum leaking out and I knew the other men could see that too. "These guys are my brothers," Scotty said. "Better than brothers, because we chose each other. We got no secrets and we share everything."

The black man unzipped his pants and brought out a huge cock that was growing hard. He took it in his hand and stroked it, then moved toward the bed. I trembled. "Everything?"

Scott bent down to kiss me. "Everything. Every damn thing."

I saw the short man took off his shirt. As he flexed his rippling muscles they made the tattoos on his arms dance obscenely.

The black man sat across from Scotty, smiling broadly. "It's gonna be fine, sweet little pussy. You gonna be so content when we done."

The short man coughed and when I looked, he was naked, his cock hard, and coming to the bed.

"I need a beer," Scotty said, and he stood, letting his jeans fall to the ground. He kicked them away. Then wearing only his vest, went into the other room, leaving me alone with his two very horny brothers.

———— ◆ ————

I was naked on the bed, unable to think as the black man stroked my thighs, then pushed them apart and crawled between my knees. My attention was riveted on his magnificent purple cock. It made me afraid and excited, and even if I'd objected, what could I do? Having let Scotty fuck me, I was in their world. The scene was nothing I would have agreed to, but no one was asking. This powerful naked man grabbed my ankle, lifted the leg high and stared into my wet and freshly fucked cunt. He smiled, grabbed his thick prick and moved forward to position it at my pussy lips. He leaned forward and the head of his huge prick pressed into me. I reached down and used my fingers to splay the lips apart.

"That's right," the man said. "Now I'll shove that pecker home sweet home."

I cried out as he rammed into me. As big as he was, Scotty had already fucked me, leaving me wet and somewhat stretched, but this guy was the biggest I'd ever had and he wasn't thinking about me. All he was thinking about was how good his cock felt as he stuffed it in my tight pussy. And, as he bent my legs back, filling me, that huge prick started feeling might good to me too.

He hooked his huge hands under my ass cheeks, lifting them and giving me more of his ebony shaft and banging steadily into me. He put his head down next to mine. I turned my face and stuck my tongue in his ear and suddenly that huge cock began to twitch in my cunt. I'd never felt anything like it. He groaned and I felt the rush of his cum spurting up inside me.

When he moved from between my sweaty thighs, I caught a glimpse of Scotty smiling in the doorway. Before the next man took his turn between my legs and blocked my view, I saw that Scotty was erect again. Watching turned him on. That probably made being brotherly a lot more fun, but it made me wonder how long this party would go on.

The short man's idea of a hot fuck was probably the most vigorous of all three of them. He threw himself into it, making me wonder if he was trying to prove something. As he bounced my ass on the bed, really pounding into me, muttering. I hooked her legs around him, wanting him to come. That took him deeper.

"Oh fuck," he moaned.

His hands pulled my ass cheeks apart and I started to think he was trying to split me in half. It wasn't the worst way to go, certainly. Despite the vigorous way he took me, fucking me so hard that sweat streamed down his cheeks, he didn't come quickly, so I began flexing my Kegel muscles, tightening my pussy around his prick.

"Oh that is nice," he moaned. It was nice to know he appreciated the effort. And he appreciated it enough that a moment later he was creaming inside me.

BANGED BY THE BIKERS

"Have a beer," Scotty said, handing me a cold bottle. I took a long pull as he sat next to me. As I drank the horny bastard fondled my breast, his fingers tugging a nipple playfully.

I drank the beer down, relishing the way it satisfied my dry mouth, then dropped the empty bottle on the floor. I sank back on the pillow looking at them and wondering what happened next. Scotty moved up the bed, coming up to sit beside me, with his back to the wall. His beautiful erect cock called to me, and reached for it, loving his smile as I wrapped my fingers around the stiff shaft, feeling its heat and knowing he wanted me.

"Roll over here and suck my cock."

With the other men watching, I rolled onto my stomach, then got on my knees in front of him, my lips touching his cock. I looked up into his eyes and watched the fire build as I caressed his prick with hand and tongue. Hands caressed my ass, stroked it. "That sure is a sweet ass." The black man sounded appreciative. It was spooky and flattering to be holding Scotty's cock up and running my tongue from its base to the tip, enjoying the tremble it induced while his friend fondled and admired my ass.

He kissed my ass, making me gasp. Then he licked it, explored my ass cheeks with his tongue and my pussy with his fingers. It was getting harder to think straight.

The short man got on the bed, kneeling over me, facing my ass. His stiff prick brushed against my belly, his hot breath warmed the small of my back and his hands touched my ass crack. Then he pulled my ass cheeks apart, exposing my anus. The black man's tongue darted down to lick it and I let out a shriek of surprise. The shock it sent through me almost made me come.

"Looks yummy," the short man said, sounding casual.

The black man teased my anus as I sucked Scotty, flicking it with his tongue while the other man held me open for him. I writhed with perverse delight and wondered if there was anything these men wouldn't do?

"You are distracting her too much. She can't give me a proper blow job," Scotty said.

The two men released me and I almost collapsed. Scotty tucked a hand under my chin and tilted my head back. "Climb on my cock and fuck me."

I stared for a moment, getting my thoughts together, then I stood, straddling his legs. Resting my hands against the wall for balance I squatted. He kissed my pussy and I lowered myself down over his prick. He grabbed his shaft and worked the tip between my pussy lips. When it was in me, he took my hips in his strong hands and forced me down on my knees, driving his cock up in me until my ass rested on him and his prick was buried neatly in my cunt.

Then he reached for my shoulders, pulling me forward and kissed me.

It might have been romantic if the black man hadn't chosen that moment to insert a wet finger in my anus, wiggling it until it slipped through my sphincter and into my rectum. I moaned and rotated my hips to grind my pussy on Scotty's cock, and the man began finger fucking my ass. As soon as I got used to the double intrusion he forced a second finger up my ass and worked the two fingers around.

In a short time even that invasion ceased hurting; the combination of sensations began to arouse me. When he pulled his fingers out, I knew what was coming. He got behind me, straddled my ass and inserted that terrible rod into my ass. "Double fuck," Scotty whooped. The pain of that ebony cock filling my back door made me cry out.

The three of us rocked together, and I was reamed by the two huge cocks inside me. Suddenly my world exploded around me. I convulsed between my two lovers. They continued fucking me, one in each hole until the cock reaming my asshole erupted, sending a fiery tsunami up my ass.

I'd almost forgotten there was a third man until he took his turn pumping his hard cock in my ass with his fierce intensity until he came. He moved away and Scotty pushed me over, lay me out flat, then crawled on my back and rammed his cock in my ass and began fucking it, seeming to go on forever. I was limp and numb, but he slid a hand under me and began to play with my clit. My head spun, and suddenly, amazingly, I came again, writhing under him. That was what he wanted. I know because he came—hard. Then I lost consciousness.

———◆———

When I woke I wasn't sure I could move. Surrounded by the smells of sex, the odors of being fucked multiple times, I heard the snores of contented men. The idea that I had fucked them all, satisfied them all, amazed me.

Sooner or later I'd have to get up and get ready for work. I needed a shower, but there was something appealing in the idea of going to work smelling of biker cum, stinking of them while serving food to other men.

I sighed. Being gang banged by bikers wasn't much of a future, but what an experience. For sure I felt better than she had a few days ago. I touched my sore pussy. Who could tell what the future held?

BANGED BY THE BIKERS

And there was still the matter of the offer of a ride on Scotty's bike. That would be some ride—I was sure of that.

PART 2

I got to the diner for my shift feeling like my world had changed — and it had. The night before I'd been fucked hard by three bikers. I'd wanted Scotty so bad, and then he'd shared me with his brothers, that big black man and the squat white guy he'd come into the diner with. It had been the wildest night of my life.

Scotty promised me a midnight ride on his bike and I was looking forward to that. We'd been too busy the night before but he wanted to show me what it was like out under the night sky on his big, bad motorcycle. "After you get off work tonight," he'd told me. "We can tear down the highway with that bad beast throbbing between our legs. You can't believe the turn on that is. We can head out of town, and when we stop I'll fuck you until you can't walk."

It sounded good to me. Unbelievably good. It was nice to have that to think about, to look forward to instead of just having to think about working the dinner to closing shift in Al's shitty diner. Al was okay, in a greasy way, but working there reminded me of how crappy life was. Except for Scotty and his pals.

BANGED BY THE BIKERS

Hilda was the other waitress that night. She's older, probably in her thirties. It was a slow night and I knew that wasn't good. On slow nights she resented me because it meant sharing the tips. She was kind of sour and I tried to stay out of her way. I even let her wait on customers at my tables sometimes, even though I needed the money as much as she did.

A couple of hours after the dinner crowd, such as it was, left, Scotty and his two pals came in. It made my pussy tingle to see them. Just looking at them conjured up hot memories of the three of them screwing me like I'd never had it before. They'd said we'd do it again, but seeing them made it real and got me wet.

"Hey babe," Scotty said as they slid into the booth. He sat at the outside and when I came over to stand beside him I felt the delicious warmth of his hand caress my bare thigh. I like that he wanted me. It made me shiver.

"You guys want something to eat?"

The black guy took the menu I handed him and licked his lips. "The tastiest thing in this place ain't even on this thing," he said. Remembering what he'd done to me the night before, having his cock in my ass, made me get wet. While my imagination ran wild, Scotty's fingers moved up under my uniform to run over my pussy. I thought I might come right there. Scotty slipped his fingers under the crotch of my panties. As I opened my legs to let him stroke my snatch, he smiled at his friends. "My fingers tell me that Carla here is looking forward to a midnight ride."

I was. "And what happens after too. But for now, how about some coffee?" I asked. "I have to work a few hours more before we play."

"Coffee then," Scotty said. "And maybe a burger and fries. I want to keep my strength up for later."

I touched his arm loving the strength I felt. Scotty had powerful muscles — especially the one between his legs. "Good thinking."

"I'm expecting some friends in a bit," he said. "Stay close. I need you to help me settle something."

That the bikes had come in made Hilda happy because the truckers who came in later gave them a wide berth and sat over in her area. Even the ones who came in to hit on me saw that the bikers were staking a claim.

Hilda knew most of the truckers — they were good tippers. But they were also guys. If the bikers hadn't been there they would've sat in my area and she'd be twiddling her thumbs. As it was, she had her customers for the night and I had mine.

Al was happy but nervous. Scotty and his friends scared him. He was probably also wondering if I'd tell Scotty that he had hit on me when I started there, tried to make me think that giving him a blowjob was a prerequisite for working there. I was pretty sure Hilda went down on him, but basically Al was harmless and he took my refusal well.

And for now we had this late little rush of business that kept Al hopping frying up burgers and making sandwiches.

I was happy to stay busy until I could get out of my stupid polyester uniform and get on that bike behind Scotty. I could imagine wrapping my arms around him as we roared down the highway. First though, I had a hunch that Scotty hadn't come early just for the coffee. When his friends came in, I was sure of it.

Some of the truckers finished their meals and left and then a family of four came in for Al's terrible meatloaf. As the family ate, Scotty got up and went to the bathroom. When he came out he wandered over to my station where Hilda and I were making coffee.

"Hey Hilda, I need for a bit," Scotty said. He slipped her a five. "Cover for her willya?"

She took the bill and put it in the pocket of her apron. "Sure." The way she looked at him I knew she wanted something besides his money.

Taking me by the arm, he led me through the kitchen

towards, Al's office. Al was at the griddle. "Hey Al, mind if I use your office for a few minutes?"

Al looked worried. "No problem."

"I won't take nothing," Scotty said. "I just want to knock off a quick piece."

He kicked the office door open and took me inside. "I can't wait for later," he told me. I faced him and he backed me up to Al's ugly desk. He'd left the door open and I could see Al peeking. Scotty didn't care. He tugged my uniform up my hips as he pushed me back on the desk and moved between my legs. "I been thinking about getting my hard prick in your sweet pussy again," he said. "Too much thinking not enough doing."

I was fumbling with the snap on his jeans, unzipping him and getting his hard cock out.

"That's right," he was saying, then he pushed me on my back on the desk. He dropped his pants and moved close, spreading my legs apart. He held one leg and his other hand went to my pussy, pushing the crotch of my panties aside. Then he was bringing that throbbing prick to it. I felt the heat of it and then he began working it between my lips. "Nice wet snatch," he said, sighing softly.

When he had the tip tucked in me he grabbed my legs, one calf in each hand, and lifted them. I saw the hungry look on his face looming between my legs, and then he thrust his hips forward.

"Oh fucking sweet," I cried as he impaled me with that thing.

The desk squeaked as it slid back and forth over the cheap assed linoleum while Scotty fucked me on it. He was worked up and it didn't take long before he just lunged forward, slamming into me. I felt the wet heat of his cum as he fired into me. He'd power into me, shooting his jizz up in my cunt, then do it again. Then, with his prick buried in me, he just stopped and held me that way while the last of his cum drained into me.

When he slipped out, dribbling cum over my thighs, he pulled up his pants. "My friends should be here any time," he said. "Let's get back out there."

As we passed back through the kitchen he slapped Al on the back. "Thanks, man."

In the diner Scotty insisted I leave my sopping wet panties on, pulled awkwardly to the side the way he'd moved them. After a time three more bikers came in. They all wore denim jackets and no shirts. "More guys from my gang," he said.

They looked the part... kind of scruffy, but hot. One

was short and dark, I thought he looked part Mexican. The others were skinheads — pasty white guys, both tall. My guess was they were real brothers, maybe twins. The twins sat in one booth and Scotty sat with the Mexican guy in another. "This is Tony," Scotty told me.

Tony was checking me out pretty good. "Scotty says you are hot as a tamale with green sauce," he told me.

"I don't eat fucking tamales, Tony," Scotty said.

"No, but you eat pussy," Tony said. He looked at me with big eyes. "That can be spicy."

The diner was mostly clearing out with all of Hilda's customers leaving. After a time, Al came out and talked with Hilda, then they called me over. "I'm going home," Al said. "Not feeling good and things are too fucking slow to believe." He nodded at my bikers. "Hilda can close when these bums are done."

"Great," I said.

Then he left.

Hilda pouted. "I have to stay, but won't even make any tips."

Scotty smiled at her. "I'll make it worth your while, Hilda." She gave him a puzzled look. "I was thinking of having a private party. Why don't you close the door, lock up right now?"

Hilda was getting the message. "Well…"

"Somebody wants in, tell them you are closed for rough trade."

One of the pasty white boys slid out of his booth to come over and stand behind Hilda. He reached around her waist and then pulled her against him putting his hand up under her uniform. She didn't protest.

"You're nice," he said. "I like smoking hot cougars. Can you growl?"

Tony was still focused on me. "Scotty owes me a favor," he said.

Scotty nodded. "I do."

He reached over and began unbuttoning my uniform. I just let him, enjoying the feel of his hands when he'd opened the top and began playing with my breasts. Then he bent over and tasted one, sucking the nipple hard. "Sweet," he said. Then he stood up and took my hand. "Why don't you and me go over to the bar?"

When he got me to my feet, he pushed my uniform down my shoulders. It's a baggy thing and I let it just fall to the ground. That left me standing there in nothing but panties and shoes and with my pussy bare.

Tony was a well-built guy and once I'd realized that Scotty intended to let him have me, I decided he'd be a good fuck. He pulled me over to the bar and sat on a stool, pulling me close to him. I put my hands on his shoulders and looked him in the eye. "What?"

"I need a blowjob," he said. "Show the crew how well you can suck my brown biker cock."

A glance at Scotty told me he expected me to do what I was told, so I reached down to Tony's crotch. He was hard… I could tell that much. I unzipped his jeans and sank to my knees, reaching in his pants. I found his hot sweet meat and wrapped my fingers around it. I had to undo the snap on his pants to get it out. It was a lovely brown shaft with a big reddish head. I pointed it up and ran my tongue up to the tip. Then I stared up into his eyes as I slowly parted my lips and then took it inside. Guys like the bedroom eyes look just before you swallow their cock.

His prick was a real mouthful.

Scotty had come over to sit on the next stool and the black guy sat down on the other side of us. "This is fine shit," Tony said. He was liking it, holding my head and letting me take him to that ragged edge. "I could come in that sweet mouth," he said.

I sucked a little harder but he pulled my head back and looked at me. "No. I want some spicy pussy wrapped around my cock." He pulled me to my feet and I could see he wanted me to straddle him. He was leaning back against the bar, so I threw a leg over him. I had my feet on the rungs of the bar stool and I put my cunt right over that nice brown prick. He held it as I lowered myself onto it.

Scotty reached over and slipped his hand down that back of my panties. So as I felt Tony's cock fill me, Scotty's fingers began playing in my ass crack and then worming a finger into my ass.

Tony was playing with my tits, sucking one and then another, or just tugging on the nipples as I started moving on him. Scotty's finger in my ass was a lovely distraction, but I was using my cunt muscles to work on Tony. He was already close from me sucking him and his eyes told me he wouldn't last long.

"Fucking hell," he cried out as his cum flooded up inside me. I wasn't the sharp eruptions Scotty had shot earlier, more like one gusher of an explosion.

When he finished, Scotty was undoing his pants. Happily he was hard again. He pulled me off Tony's lap and turned me to face away from him. "Take off the panties," he said. When I bent over he pulled me against him, my back to him. I barely got my panties off before he lifted me up with my legs in the air. I reached for his cock and he grabbed my ass and lowered me. I guided him inside again with a sigh. But then he lifted me again. "Put that in your ass," he said. "I'm going to bugger you my sweet cunt."

I reached down and found his slippery cock and

pointed it back where he wanted it. It was a jolt as my own weight pulled me down on it, as it stretched my tight anus. I cried out. It hurt but it felt good too and Scotty wanted to fuck my ass, so it was good.

I used my feet on the rungs to control our motion a little and worked his cock into my ass. Then, when I was taking all of it, the black guy got in front of me and dropped his pants. That beautiful ebony tool was jutting out, wanting my pussy. He stepped on the rungs of the stool and Scotty reached around, grabbing my tits and pulling me back. The black man brought his cock to my pussy and drove it home.

I wrapped my legs around his hard body and looked at his face, his hungry eyes; I almost couldn't believe I was being double fucked again.

The black guy provided all the action. Scotty was just holding me. "I can feel his prick in your cunt," he whispered in my ear as the black guy started getting rougher, banging me hard. Sweated beaded on his forehead and his eyes were wild.

Suddenly I lost it. "I'm coming," I told them, my lovers, and I was. My body was loving the friction of two hard cocks and I began thrashing, writhing, my cunt squeezing the black cock.

"Oh fuck," the black guy moaned, and then he was

coming too. That warm rush of his come with Scotty stuck up my ass was incredible.

As he moved away, the stocky white guy with tattoos was there to take his place. He'd taken his clothes off and he rammed his hard cock into my squishy, wet hole. I hooked my legs around him and he went to it. He must've been watching for a time, because he came fast.

Keeping his cock in my ass, Scotty slipped off the barstool and turned me to face the bar. I slumped over it as he began seriously fucking my ass. He needed to come and he slapped my ass periodically. The blows stung, but they were also sexy and the way Scotty was reaming out my asshole was making my entire body tremble.

Then he was shooting his thick, creamy jizz up my backside and I was melting into the bar.

———◆———

I slumped at the bar feeling cum trickling out of my pussy and ass. I could hear Hilda whimpering somewhere, but I had no idea where she was or who was doing what to her. I didn't care much either. The two pale white guys were on either side of me. They had both taken off their pants and their stiff pricks were ready for action.

They turned me around so that my back was to the bar

and each grabbed a tit. They took my hands and put them on their stiff cocks. "Stroke them, girlie," one said.

When I did I realized that both of them had studs in the heads of their cocks, through the glans. I don't know the names of the piercings guys do, but they each had a bar that ran the same direction as the cock. One of them had a gold ring piercing his scrotum. I guess that was one way to tell them apart.

One of them pushed my head down to his crotch. "Taste test," he muttered and I took it in my mouth as the other one spread my ass cheeks apart and poked his cock into my wet snatch.

I expected to feel the piercing, but it didn't feel much different than any other cock, so maybe he got the benefit of that thing. I was there between these two, sucking one long pale cock while taking the other in my cunt. They fucked me that way for a time before swapping me end for end and making me taste my pussy on the one cock while the other stuffed my cunt.

When they swapped again, the one fucking me pulled out after just a couple of strokes. "Nice and wet," he said. I guessed what was coming but I was concentrating on sucking the cock in my mouth when the one behind me rammed his cock up my ass. Even after Scotty doing my ass it stretched me. Then the guy bent over me and wrapped long pale arms around me and straightened up, lifting me off my feet.

As I went up, the other guy grinned and grabbed my legs. He locked them under his arms, holding me. My own weight was pushing me down on his brother's hard prick, spreading my asshole open with that meaty shaft. I sank down, making more of his prick burn its way up my asshole. The guy in front, grinning ear to ear, moved close between my legs and guided his cock to my pussy. I sighed as he impaled me with it and I locked my legs around his waist, tucking it all up there.

Then the two of them were bouncing me up and down so that their cocks moved together inside me. It was a different way of getting double penetrated.

"Holy shit, that's sweet," the guy with his prick in my ass was saying. His brother said nothing — his face was tense, eyes wide.

"Bang that ass and pussy," the black man said.

He and the other man were watching and stroking their cocks. The line had formed.

Amazingly the twins even came at just about the same time. It was amazing taking cum up my ass and cunt at the same time. Amazing in a crazy wonderful way.

The black guy grabbed me and pulled me close to him then he faced me away from him, bent me over, and stuffed my ass with his prick. I moaned and the tattooed guy grabbed my hair and fed his hard cock into my open mouth.

The guy's cock tasty musky and I wondered if he'd fucked Hilda, if I was tasting her pussy. While I sucked the tattooed biker the other guy made sure I knew what it felt like to take every inch of his long, black prick up my well-lubricated asshole.

It felt mighty good and as he drove his iron piston into that hole, his buddy enjoyed what my mouth and tongue could do to his cock. He was taking over, more fucking my face than letting me suck him, and that was a little hard on my lips. They'd be bruised in the morning.

I didn't give a shit.

Suddenly my mouth was filling with salty jizz. He moaned and pulled his throbbing cock out of my mouth. Thick, creamy shots of cum splattered over my face. He held my hair and tipped my head back, getting off on watching it run down my cheeks and dribble off my chin. "Bitchin'," he said.

"I'm coming," the black guy said, and boy was he coming. The way it felt shooting up my ass and I thought it would come out my mouth it went so far. As he came he slammed that long cock up my butt. "Creaming in her rectum, man, what a deal."

BANGED BY THE BIKERS

Later I found Scotty in a booth, resting and drinking a beer. I sat beside him and he licked my face. "Hot bitch," he said. "When we go for a ride, I'm going to show you some real down and dirty."

"I can hardly wait," I said. And I meant it.

He grabbed my hair and pushed my face into his lap. It smelled like sex. "Lick my cock clean. Pussy juice gets itchy when it dries." I did and somehow it was getting this dude hard again. "I love the way you do that," he said. As if I couldn't tell. After a bit he pulled my head up. I took the swelling shaft in my hand and looked at him, wanting him to tell me what I should do, what would turn him on. He grinned. "Anything," I said.

"I made a promise I need to keep," he said. Then he led me over to where Hilda was stretched out in a booth, face down. She'd been royally used and looked limp. Scotty, hiked her ass up in the air. He spread her ass cheeks apart and showed me her anus. "Practical new," he laughed, then he leaned over and spit right in the center of that chocolate star. "I want you to lick my balls while I fuck her ass," he told me and he stood behind her, holding her ass open. "Put my cock in that little crinkled spot first."

Hilda moaned. "My ass…"

"I'm going to bugger you. You like playing cougar, this is what your hot studs need."

I took his stiff cock and pointed it where he wanted, watching the way the head spread those muscles. It was a tight fit and Scotty pushed hard. Hilda cried out when he popped the head in her. "My balls," he said.

I squatted behind him and held his big hairy sack in my hand as I ran my tongue over it. I could feel the balls inside the sack. It was tricky to move with him as he worked his prick into Hilda's ass. She was writhing and screaming as he did her. I had a great views of him burying that mighty thing in her butt the way he'd done mine.

"Rim his ass," the black man said. "That'll make him come. Spread his ass cheeks and lick his butthole."

"Yes," Scotty said.

So I found myself prying his ass cheeks apart. I saw the line that ran from his balls up his crack and I traced it with my tongue. His butt was tangy, almost acid, but I forced myself to lick it as best I could with him thrusting his hips, driving his pecker into Hilda's ass. I wanted him to come, so I started working a finger into his ass, licking it, getting it wet, and pushing it in his asshole and wiggling it around. Then I worked in a second finger and while I fucked his asshole with my fingers I used my other hand to work his balls into my mouth and I sucked those eggs.

Then he came. I felt him shudder, his balls tighten, and he emptied himself in her ass.

———◆———

We went out into the parking lot. It was cool and I hadn't been able to find my panties.

One of the pasty guys was helping Hilda to her car. He'd locked up for her and put the keys in her purse. I looked over at Scotty's bike feeling good. I'd been gangbanged by this bunch twice and now I'd get my ride. And maybe fucked more. It was a glorious night.

Then Scotty's cell phone rang. "What the fuck?" He listened. "Okay. Right away." He turned to the guys. "Apple's place. Trouble with the WestWing Riders."

"What is it?" I asked.

"Some guys from another gang cornered some of our people. We need to rescue their dumb asses. Sorry babe. We have to make the ride for later. Don't worry, I'll be back when we settle this beef."

I kissed him and then watched as they started their bikes and roared out of the parking lot. As I walked to my car feeling sorry for myself, I saw Hilda in hers, slumped over the wheel. I think she was sound asleep. I smiled. She'd gotten more than she bargained for. I smiled. Even though the idea of driving home in my crappy car and sleeping alone made me sad, I'd gotten more than I'd hoped for and soon I'd get my ride on the back of that big, nasty bike. And then that big, nasty biker would ride me hard.

PART 3

The problem with getting hooked on bikers is they are pretty wild. That's the good part too, of course, but it had been three days since I'd last seen Scotty and his crew. I knew they had club business, dealing with a rival club, but sitting around waiting to hear from him again was hard. And who knew when they'd be back

Meantime my life was fucking dull and worse, I was horny.

The job at the diner sucked. I needed the money it paid but hated the work. And now I'd tasted a more exciting life -- being a biker bitch, Scotty's biker bitch. Even though Scotty's idea of love involved letting his buddies gang bang me, I was pining for more.

Besides, Scotty had promised me a ride on his bike. It had already been postponed twice now, and I wanted it to happen. But it was hard to be patient.

I got myself ready for work, as ready as you can when you have to wear a crappy polyester uniform that looks like it was made for a dumpy nurse. I decided to postpone the downer feeling I get putting it on, and wear shorts and a halter top to work and change in the bathroom. Once I met Scotty I had decided that if I wanted to be a biker groupie I should dress like one and the shorts and halter top, with heels, seemed about right. They were very short shorts and fit tight.

I couldn't do much about my car though. So I got in and let it rattle and clank me all the way to the diner. It's a good thing New Mexico doesn't have smog inspections as I couldn't afford a car that would pass.

I parked at the edge of the parking lot where there was a good and working street light. It was already getting dark and I worked until two in the morning. I might get hot for bikers, but even I worry about some of the creeps who eat at Al's diner. I've had one try to jump my bones out there. Scotty fixed his ass.

As I walked to the diner I heard a whistle. I turned and my heart skipped a beat. "Scotty." And there he was, sitting astride his brilliant blue chopper, in jeans, boots and a vest.

"I was waiting for you, cunt. Want to take that ride now?"

That was the sweetest thing I'd ever heard.

"I'm supposed to work."

He shrugged. "You can go in a work for Al, or you can come with me." Then he put his hands on his hips. "I was thinking about taking you on a long ride. A dirty ride. One that you might not come back from."

"Not come back?"

He winked. "If you can deal with me and my friends, there's no reason you ever need to go to Al's again." He nodded toward my car. "Or drive that piece of shit again."

My heart raced. "You want me to go with you."

He put a hand behind him and patted the seat. "That's what I said. We can see what happens."

I looked at the uniform I was carrying. I had a job and Scotty was asking me to toss that away for a ride on his motorcycle and a hard fuck. I turned and tossed my uniform in the trash can outside the door. "Let's go."

No matter how it worked out, this was too good to pass up.

———◆———

Finally, I was slipping onto the seat behind Scotty, putting my arms around his waist. He kicked the beast into life and the rumble of the engine sent a thrill rippling through me that was as exciting as the first time a guy felt me up. No shit. I had my feet on pegs and I pressed my face against his back as he put it in gear and we surged forward, heading out of the parking lot.

The diner sat off the freeway on a frontage road and

Scotty took the onramp up onto the four lane road accelerating all the way. I'd never felt anything like it, with the wind whipping at us. I was sure I'd be peeled right off and I grabbed hold of his leather belt. He zipped in and out of cars, and then ducked off the main road to road down a two lane asphalt road with no street lights. The dashed white line marking the center of the road danced in the glow of our headlight and a slim crescent moon.

I was in heaven. The asphalt below us flew by inches away and that bike seemed to go wherever Scotty pointed it, defying gravity and yet glued to the road. The steady throb of the engine was getting my pussy wet and the feel of his hard body against my breasts and face was intoxicating. As we rode the sensation that I'd blow off faded and the heat factor grew. I was excited, wet, and the hand that gripped Scotty's belt moved down to cup the bulge in his jeans.

The man was hard.

I watched the shadowy buildings and trees alongside the road blur by as I undid Scotty's belt, then unsnapped his jeans. I fumbled getting his zipper down but when I did I uncoiled that rubbery snake and held it in my hand.

He moaned softly and I realized I was stroking his prick. I glanced at the speedometer. It said seventy five. He was worked up and that meaty shaft of his grew rigid. We wobbled a little as I jerked him off, feeling like this had to be the most exciting thing in the world. Then he came. His cock twitched in my hand, his cum splattered over my hand, over his jeans, and blew by me.

"Bitchin'," he said. I held onto his cock as it softened.

A few miles down the road, he pulled into an abandoned gas station. It was almost falling down. He pulled into the garage and stopped. He left the engine running as we got off. He grabbed me and undid my shorts, yanking them down, taking my panties with them. When I kicked them off my feet, he got at the end of the bike, put me on the seat facing him, and hooked my legs over his shoulders. I fell back as he pressed his face to my pussy and began licking me savagely. He used his fingers to probe inside me as he sucked and licked my tender cunt flesh and capture my clit. He sucked my clit in his mouth and flicked it with his tongue.

All the time the engine rumbled with its enormous power, adding that pulsing, throbbing vibration to the humming of my body as it danced to the tune played by his fingers and tongue.

And then I came.

"Stupid bitch, you coulda got us killed."

"Who fucking cares?" I said. "I was jerking off my biker at seventy five miles per hour."

He laughed. "Your sweet ass was meant for a bike."

When we got back on the bike he ran up on the freeway again. There wasn't much traffic. The road was practically deserted. He didn't say where we were going, and I didn't ask. We were out in the open desert, headed west toward Gallup on I-40. What else did I need to know? I'd decided to go with Scotty as far as that went and I didn't even know what town he was from.

After some time we stopped for coffee and sandwiches at a truck stop then were back on the road. When he pulled into a rest stop he led me to one of the little shelters where there's a picnic table. The light was out in this one and came up behind me and undid my shorts again. "Fucking cunt," he muttered as he dropped my pants and panties, squatting to tug them down and nipping my ass cheeks with his teeth. With my shorts and panties around my ankles, I bent forward for him and he thrilled me by lapping my pussy again. Then he stood and put one hand on my back. His other was undoing his pants. The sound of the zipper on his jeans coming down sent a shiver of anticipation running through me.

Then he was poking his prick between my pussy lips,

working it in. I was still goddamn wet, and him licking me had made me hotter. He stroked that bitching prick into me and I moaned with how good it felt. But he was just getting set up. He pulled out of me, then shoved it in again. The next time he pressed it to my anus. Scotty has rammed his tool up there more than once. "I want to see if this hole is as tight as I remember it," he said and then I gasped as he rammed it in hard.

He held a handful of hair at the back of my head and tipped my head back as he fucked my ass. "A good bitch takes it in the ass and loves it," he said. "Are you a good bitch, Carla?"

"Fuck my ass hard, you bastard."

"I thought so."

He was ramming it into me and I put one hand down between my legs to play with my pussy. His cock felt fantastic in my ass, but this was even better — me fiddling my clit while he reamed my ass. His balls slapped against my hand; that was cool too, feeling those great big balls that way.

Then he came, and his cum burned its way up my rectum. Just as he was shooting off, I came, with me moaning and twitching. "Yes, milk that cock." He was happy.

The rest of the trip didn't take long. He got off the freeway in a smallish city I didn't know and went straight to a bar. I figured it was his hangout as the parking lot was filled with kick ass motorcycles. Outside the bar some guys were smoking joints while one of them got a blowjob from a blonde who'd seen better days. She was skinny and kind of haggard looking.

"Henry," he said. "For Henrietta. She's a club whore."

"Whore?"

"She hangs around, guys buy her drinks, give her dope, a place to sleep… in return she does whoever wants her. She was the old lady of one of the top guys until he played stupid with a semi and got himself and a perfectly good bike squashed flat."

"Shit."

"She was too far past her 'use by' date to get another guy, and hooked on this life."

He led me inside the bar, which wasn't crowded, but busy. The jukebox played sixties rock. I recognized the guys who'd been with Scotty at the diner during his last two trips. The pasty skin-headed twins were taking turns screwing a girl in the corner, fucking her against the wall.

"A groupie," Scotty said.

"And me? What am I?"

We sat at a table and he was close to me. "How about being my old lady?"

"Your old lady?"

"You ride with me, live with me, but you do what I say."

The idea made me quiver. Scotty was rough, but I liked him. Being his old lady meant I wouldn't ever have to go back to that shitty life, the diner, my crap car. "I'd like that."

"You do who I say too."

"Like before? You let your buddies have me?"

"Right. Are you cool with that?"

"I am."

He grinned. "Well, I think we will be putting that to the test."

A big man with shaggy black hair came walking over to our table. Beside him a slim black girl carried a tray of full beer mugs. "Hey Scotty," the man said. The closer he came the bigger he looked.

"Mason," Scotty said. "This here is Carla."

As Della put beers in front of us, Mason sat down beside me. He lifted his glass. "You guys did a good job the other day, Scotty. They won't be back soon."

"I hope not. We lost Hector."

"Acceptable losses," Mason said. "Not easy or pleasant, but that's the way shit goes down." He took a long drink then looked me up and down. "You are new around here, Carla," he said. "Fresh."

I liked the look of him. "Just arrived from Albuquerque."

"She looks tired," Della said.

"And tasty," Mason said. He put his hand in my lap, doing it openly so Scotty saw plain enough. I took my cue from Scotty who just leaned back and took a long drink of his beer. "Tired but tasty." He winked at Scotty. "And what is Carla doing in a rough-assed biker bar with a hard case like Scotty?"

He was intimidating but I didn't want to show it. I nodded toward Scotty. "Hanging out with the hard case isn't enough?"

Mason laughed. "It depends on whether you know what you are in for."

"Mason is president of the club," Scotty said. "He's the exception."

"To what?"

"To everything."

Mason grinned. "The club pays my bar tab. They pay my rent. I fuck any bitch that gets my prick hard."

BANGED BY THE BIKERS

I could see where this was going easy enough. "You want to be Scotty's old lady, you are going to be mine too. I like fucking rough and raw." He took my hand and put it on the large bulge in his crotch. "You want to be his old lady, then you gotta let me throw a little welcome party with you as the centerpiece -- the piece in the fucking center of it." He laughed at his joke.

I looked at Scotty. "That's how it works." He reached over and lifted up my halter top, pulling it over my head, then tossed it aside. "I want Carla as my old lady," he said. The words made me shiver. Even with everyone watching, I didn't care what I had to do to get that title. Mason stared at me expectantly, so I swallowed and then let my fingers find his zipper. He leaned back, smiling as I pulled it down. "I better find out for myself if she's good enough for you Scotty. I better see how she takes it in every hole."

He laughed and grabbed my face in his large hand. "I like spirited cunts," he said. He held my face tight, hurting me, showing off. I didn't fight him. Instead I finished undoing his pants and getting his cock out. It was big, like the rest of him and I wrapped my fingers around it. "Then what's your pleasure, Mr. President?"

He slid his chair back. "Start by showing everyone that you have tasted my presidential cock."

I bent my face down and licked the head of his prick,

running my tongue around it, then opening my mouth wide to take it inside. He rested his huge hand on my head and controlled the pace as I started sucking him off with the whole bar coming around to watch. "The girl is a decent cocksucker," Mason announced. Then he grabbed my hair and stood, pulling me off his cock and to my feet. He grabbed a tit with each hand. "Take off the shorts," he said. He watched me undo them, and then released me as I slid them and my panties down to all sorts of whistles and cat calls. When I was standing there is nothing but heels, he pushed me back on the table. The gang moved in around me. I couldn't see Scotty. Hands grabbed at my tits and ran over my belly as Mason dropped his pants, then lifted my legs up, looking at my pussy. He poked his hard cock into my cunt, then scooted me closer and leaned into me, driving that prick deep.

The table rocked as he fucked me. Two guys I didn't know sucked on my nipples for a time, then one undid his pants and rubbed his hard cock over my tit. "Cool," the other guy said and he did the same, but he rubbed his over my cheek.

"Fuck the bitch's face," Mason said, and the guy whose cock was on my cheek grabbed my head, turning it sideways to face his crotch. He forced his cock in my mouth, putting a hand on his hip and fucking my mouth.

BANGED BY THE BIKERS

The guy rubbing his cock on my breast suddenly moaned and shot creamy cum over my tits. As he moved away another guy, another stiff prick took his place.

Then Mason came. He roared like some damn animal and I could feel the spurts of cum he shot in my pussy. It was a lot of cum and, just before he finished, he pulled out and stroked his cock, spending the rest on my belly. The guy fucking my face laughed at that, and he pulled out. "Suck my balls," he said, pushing them into my mouth. As I did, he shot off on my, spraying his cream down my body. Another guy was between my legs and I saw it was Tony, the Mexican guy in Scotty's crew shoving his prick in my cunt. A black guy decided to fuck my mouth and two other guys put my hands on their hard pricks, expecting me to jerk them off while their buddies did me.

I was surrounded by hard, throbbing pricks, and they would come, usually on me, and be replaced by a fresh one. I was losing count of them. Tony flooded me with his jizz and was replaced by another guy.

Then I was being moved, turned. I saw Mason standing there, giving orders, stroking his huge prick. It was hard and I knew what was coming as they put my feet on the floor and bent me face down over the table. Two guys held my arms as Mason got behind me. Other hands spread my ass cheeks apart and I moaned as the head of that big thick prick pressed into my anus. I cried out as he rammed that hard cock up my ass. I was glad Scotty had butt fucked me earlier, because Mason gave it all to me in one hard thrust that made my head spin.

Mason's fingers dug into my hips as he fucked my ass furiously. The room was a blur. Sweat and cum were in my eyes. Cum drying all over my body made me feel weird, but that cock pounding in my ass was the center of my universe. I could ignore the hands on my ass, the hard cocks brushing against my face. I barely noticed when a couple of the guys came over my back, shooting their gooey cum over me.

Then Mason's hot cum shot up my ass. His hands were like a vise on my hips as he held my butt against him and emptied his balls in me. As he moved away, dribbling cum on my thighs, someone scooped me up and carried me to another table. Another big biker lay on his back on it, naked, his cock jutting up. They put me over him, setting my cunt down over his cock. Then another one straddled my ass, standing on the table. His cock jabbed into my ass and I had them both fucking me, one in each hole while other guys watched, jerking off, coming on my face, on my tits.

The guy in my ass didn't last long and another took his place. I was having trouble breathing and I was exhausted.

Then, somehow, it stopped. The guy under me came and rolled me off him. The squat, tattooed guy from Scotty's crew pulled my legs down and rammed his cock in my ass a few times, then came over my ass cheeks.

Then I was lying on the table… alone.

————◆————

Della came and got me, taking me into the back of the bar. There was a shower there and she stripped down and helped me wash. Then she put me on a bed, covered me with a blanket and let me sleep.

When I woke, Della brought me a beer and a sandwich. "You okay?" she asked.

"Sore, wiped out. Overly fucked, but okay."

"I know the feeling," she said. Her look told me that she did.

"Did I pass?"

She grinned. "Pretty much. There is still a private ceremony though. Rest some more. The guys are still out."

I did and the next time I woke to see Scotty and Mason coming in the room. Della came behind them. They were all naked.

"You're a hot bitch," Mason said, sitting on the bed. "You should be good for Scotty, and I'll like having you around. I just need to see one last thing. Being gang banged is one thing, but are you going to do what you are told?"

"Sure."

"Fine." He waved at Della and Scotty and they got on the bed. "Get my cock throbbing hard, then I want you to beg me to fuck Della's ass. Make it sound like you really want me to enjoy a nice butt fuck in some other bitch."

That didn't seem so bad, so I tossed off the covers and began doing exactly that. I held his balls and sucked his cock, trying to make sure I didn't overdo it. Della was lying on her stomach with her legs apart and Scotty was playing with her pussy lips. I took him out of my mouth and stroked his shaft. "Why don't you fuck that cute ass, Mason? Bugger Della. I'll bet that would make your cock feel so fucking good."

"Show me her asshole," he said. I moved over and spread her ass cheeks apart and there was that sweet, crinkled hole. "Put a finger in it," he said.

I wet a finger in my mouth and forced it in through those tight little muscles. "It's so fucking tight, Mason."

He moved up over her, bracing himself with a hand on either side of her and getting on his knees between her legs. I held his throbbing cock and guided it to her butt. Mason lowered himself and then drove it into the girl. She cried out as he impaled her.

As he started pounding into her, Scotty pulled me close, wrapping his arms around me and cupping my breasts. Somehow, despite all that was going on, that made me feel safe. We watched Mason driving his long cock into Della's asshole, seeing the way her black ass cheeks moved — it was sexy. I was gently stroking Scotty's prick the whole time, running a nail over the tip, teasing, then backing off.

Finally Mason came. He held his cock in her ass, then pulled out and shot more cum over her ass cheeks.

"You want your old man to enjoy some of that don't you?" he asked me.

I turned to Scotty. "Want to fuck that black ass, Scotty. I bet you'd love coming in her back door."

"Sweet," he said. Then he knelt behind her, pulling her onto her knees. I put his cock in Della's stretched butt hole and Mason got behind me to feel me up as we watched Scotty ram into Della's back door.

When Scotty came, he shot some over the girl's ass too.

"Now," Mason said. "A good old lady, a biker chick who has encouraged her old man to butt fuck some cunt, would show him she enjoyed it. She'd want to see if she could excite him again. So I want you to lick her asshole and ass cheeks clean of our cum."

He pulled the girl up to her knees and motioned for me to get over behind her.

I moved slowly, but I knelt behind her. I put my face to her ass and began licking their salty jizz from her ass cheeks and working my way to her anus, which was all stretched out and filled with cum. I poked my tongue into it, tasting the tangy sting of her butt hole mixed with creamy cum.

"Very good, Carla," Mason said.

Mason got up and grabbed Della's hand. "Welcome to the club," he said. "As Scotty's old lady you have full membership privileges. You'll fuck me when I want it, but other than that, unless it's someone Scotty approves, anyone hassles you and we will beat his ass. As club president I pronounce you his old lady. You may now suck his dick… or do whatever he wants you to do."

Scotty's big, nasty bike screamed as we roared down the highway. It was dark and the headlight illuminated things strangely on the back road, making it spooky. That I was perched on back stark naked was fucking hot… crazy, strange, smoking hot.

When we left the bar, me as Scotty's old lady, he had

me walk through the bar naked. It wasn't like the sight of my body was anything new to any of these guys, but he was asserting himself, showing them I was his. I had my face covered in his cum. We'd gone out to his bike and I got on behind him, naked and he'd stood that bike on its ass when we left the parking lot. I had to hang onto him for dear life.

Now I was leaking cum onto the leather seat and letting my hands dance over his crotch as his brilliant blue bike roared through the dark, sending its erotic throbbing pulse through me. My pussy and ass were still sore from the gang bang, but unbelievably this ride, this magical flying through the dark was getting me horny again.

"We'll stop down the road aways," he told me. "Then we'll go down to Mexico. I want to fuck you on the beach."

I knew Scotty wouldn't wait until we got to some beach to fuck me. The place we were stopping was a biker hangout too, and he hadn't made me ride naked just to scare the tourists.

"I have some friends down the road I want you to meet," he told me. "My old buddy Johnny Liquor has a smoking hot old lady. She's Chinese. She can give you some new clothes. Best of all, we can have a little party, the four of us. You'll like them; they're downright crazy.

She goes nuts when Johnny has another chick go down on her while he watches."

I could tell Scotty thought of that as classy entertainment too. So soon enough I'd get fucked by another of Scotty's pals and probably have to eat his old lady's pussy. Meantime, I had his hard cock in my hand, stroking it while we roared past farms and dark hills. Either I'd make him come with my hand, or he'd pull over and fuck me in some hole. It didn't matter much. With Scotty I could count on doing it all.

And then we'd ride to the next adventure.

˜ THE END ˜

ABOUT THE AUTHOR

Dear Reader,

Thanks for reading one of my filthy tales! My name is Lolita Minx and chances are, as you're reading this, I'm up to absolutely no good. My man, Gary, and I have a special arrangement: we experiment, with ourselves, each other, and a whole bunch of other people whether known to us or complete strangers. Anything goes, there are no rules, except one: we have to have fun. For me, there's an extra layer of fun after the all the decadence and depravity has taken place. I like to write down our experiences, and share them with the world. Check back soon for more dirty tales as I finish writing them ;-)

My stories are available at all major ebook retailers, most have been made into audiobooks as well. You can visit my website for more details.

To find out more, check:

eXplicitTales.com

(And why not sign up for the newsletter to be the first to find out about new releases.)

x Lolita

9 781913 930424